Sesame Street
A Christmas Treasury

❄ **A Sesame Street Christmas** ❄
❄ **Merry Christmas, Everybody!** ❄
❄ **A Grouch's Christmas** ❄

Sesame Street
A Christmas Treasury

❋ **A Sesame Street Christmas** ❋

❋ **Merry Christmas, Everybody!** ❋

❋ **A Grouch's Christmas** ❋

FEATURING JIM HENSON'S SESAME STREET MUPPETS

A GOLDEN BOOK

Published by Golden Books Publishing Company, Inc.,
in conjunction with Children's Television Workshop

A portion of the money you pay for this book goes to Children's Television Workshop.
It is put right back into SESAME STREET and other CTW educational projects. Thanks for helping!

A Sesame Street
Christmas

By **Pat Tornborg**
Illustrated by **Tom Cooke**

FEATURING JIM HENSON'S SESAME STREET MUPPETS

Christmas was just a week away and it was raining when I splashed into the park. I found the gang from Sesame Street gathered under Big Bird's umbrella.

"Why all the long faces?" I asked.

"I can't build my Bert snow man," said Ernie.

"I can't count the snowflakes," said the Count.

"Me no eat snow cones," said Cookie Monster.

And then everyone nodded and looked miserable. So, I said, "This is just great! Nobody has any of that Christmas spirit they're always nagging me about! It's going to be a damp and gloomy holiday, after all. Whoopee!"

But Betty Lou didn't agree with me. She said, "Not so fast, Oscar! We're not giving up on Christmas spirit yet! Come on, everybody. Let's go to my house for some milk and cookies."

Aw, all this Christmas spirit jazz is making me sick. Big Bird, you take over.

Sure, Oscar. So we went to Betty Lou's house and everyone ate six cookies, and drank two glasses of milk, and felt a little cheerier.

"Who cares about the rain?" said Bert.

"Let's have a terrific Christmas, anyway!" said Ernie.

"Let's sing Christmas carols and tell stories!" said Betty Lou.

I said, "Sure! I can read you a Christmas poem right now. My Granny Bird reads it to me every Christmas. It's about the time there was too much snow for Christmas. Listen."

THE NIGHT BEFORE CHRISTMAS
ON SESAME STREET

'Twas the night before Christmas on Sesame Street.
And a stormy one, too, with the snow and the sleet!
All the kids in the neighborhood, snug in pajamas,
Were saying good-night to their papas and mamas.

The house was all quiet at Ernie and Bert's,
As they climbed into bed in their cozy nightshirts.
And even outside, everyone was at rest—
The grouch in his can and I in my nest.

There was one little house where not all was so comfy—
'Twas the home of that famous magician named Mumfie.
He feared that the blizzard would keep Santa away,
And he thought of a bleak Christmas morn with dismay.

"This storm might be too much for Santa," he said,
"So I'll conjure some toys for the children instead."
Then he snatched up his wand, and before he could say,
"A la Peanut Butter Sandwiches!" he was on his way.

A little past midnight, Ernie jumped out of bed.
He'd been jolted awake by a "thump" overhead.
As he peered at the roof, he said, "Gee, Bert, that's funny.
I thought Santa had reindeer, but that looks like a bunny!"

Ernie raced to the living room, just as a foot
Had emerged from the chimney all covered with soot.
The body that followed was equally grubby.
Said Ernie, "Why, this Santa's not even chubby!

"His face is all dirty, his cloak's black as night.
But I always thought Santa wore red and white!
He has only a stick poking out of his pouch,
And these gifts should have gone to Oscar the Grouch!"

Ernie hopped back in bed and was soon sound asleep,
But poor Mumford had other appointments to keep.
With his team of white rabbits, the brave little wizard
Continued his trip through the terrible blizzard.

Mumfie's magic did wonders on that Christmas Eve,
But the gifts it created were hard to believe!
There was seed for a bird by the Count's Christmas tree,
And the sneakers for me were only size three!

Little Grover had hoped for a new teddy bear,
But his gift was a ribbon for Betty Lou's hair.
And if you think that Grover was pretty unlucky,
Bert's soap dish was intended for poor Rubber Duckie!

As the morning came, Mumford drove home through
    the drifts.
He had made all his rounds, given everyone gifts.
So imagine his shock when he walked in to see
A fat, jolly old man sitting there by his tree!

"Mumford, my friend," Santa said with a smile,
"I've been two steps behind you for quite a long while.
Though you made some unusual gift selections,
You've done a fine job (with my little corrections).

"I followed your sleigh and erased all your traces.
You left all the right gifts, but in all the wrong places!
I just made a few switches, so no one would know
That old Santa Claus was held up by the snow.

"But the meaning of Christmas is not gifts, my boy;
It's the impulse to do things that bring others joy!
Though your magical wand can't do anything right,
The true magic of Christmas was with you tonight!"

With a nod of his head and a wink of his eye,
Santa hopped in his sleigh and took off for the sky.
He was heard to exclaim, as he flew out of sight,
          "A LA PEANUT BUTTER SANDWICHES!
                AND TO ALL, A GOOD-NIGHT!"

SANTA'S HELPER

When I finished reading the poem,
Betty Lou said, "Thanks for that poem,
Big Bird. Now I'm not worried about the rain or the snow."
Then Grover said, "Oh, neither am I! Christmas is
Christmas, whatever the weather!"
And I think Grover was right. Don't you?

No, Bird, I don't think Grover was right. Christmas is much better when the weather is crummy! Anyhow, I've got my own Christmas story to tell. I call it "Oscar's Christmas Carol (A Dickens of a Story)." Now, listen!

OSCAR'S CHRISTMAS CAROL
(A Dickens of a Story)

"BAH, HUMBUG!" I said loudly, just as Big Bird and Betty Lou walked by. "BAH, HUMBUG!" I said again, as they stopped to stare.

"Whatever that means, it sure sounds grouchy!" said Betty Lou. "What's the matter, Oscar?"

"Nothing's the matter," I answered. "Everything's great. I'm reading a terrific story about a mean old fellow named Mr. Scrooge. He hated Christmas, so he said, 'Bah, Humbug!' all the time. He sounds just like my uncle Smarmy. Why, he might even be a relative of mine!"

"How could anyone hate Christmas?" asked Betty Lou. "Everyone is good and kind at Christmas, and there are good things to eat, and songs to sing, and presents to give. Christmas is a happy time, Oscar."

"Bah, Humbug!" I replied.

"Mr. Scrooge had a way of fixing that. Not only was he miserable himself, but he ruined everyone else's Christmas, too. He even made his helper, Bob Cratchit, work on Christmas Eve! Boy, that's a real grouch for you!"

"Hey, wait a minute," said Bird. "I know that story. It's 'A Christmas Carol,' by Mr. Charles Dickens. Maria read it to me last Christmas. And guess what, Oscar? It has a happy ending!"

"How could it?" I asked. I was disgusted. "This guy Scrooge was such a great grouch! He's my hero—an inspiration! I want to be just like him."

"Well, then," said Bird, "you'll have to stop being a grouch, because that's what Scrooge did. He had a dream that showed him how wrong he had been about Christmas. You should read the rest of the book, Oscar."

And I said, "BAH, HUMBUG!" as I disappeared into my trash can.

I HATE CHRISTMAS

I can't think of anything that's dumber;
To a grouch, Christmas is a bummer.

Beaming faces everywhere,
Happiness is in the air.
I'm telling you it isn't fair.
I hate Christmas!

People loaded with good will,
Giving presents—what a thrill!
That slushy nonsense makes me ill.
I hate Christmas!

I'd rather have a holiday
Like normal grouches do.
Instead of getting presents,
They take presents back from you!

Here comes Santa, girls and boys.
So who needs that big red noise?
I'll tell him where to leave his toys.
I hate Christmas!
(And if you want the truth, I ain't so crazy
about Easter and Labor Day, either!)

Christmas carols to be sung,
Decorations to be hung.
Oh yeah, well I stick out my tongue!
I hate Christmas!

Christmas bells play loud and strong,
Hurts my ears, all that ding-dong.
Besides, it goes on much too long!
I hate Christmas!

I'd rather have a holiday
With a lot less joy and flash.
With a lot less cheerful smiling
And a lot more dirty trash. Yeah!

Christmas Day is almost here.
When it's over, then I cheer.
I'm glad it's only once a year!
I hate Christmas!

And whoever hung that mistletoe
over my trashcan, Well, I say,
"PHOOEY and BAH, HUMBUG!"

A little later, Bird passed my trash can on his way home from Betty Lou's house. I shouted, "Merry Christmas, Bird!" as I popped out of the can.

So, Bird looked at me in surprise. He said, "Why, Oscar, you changed your mind. You must have had a dream, just like Mr. Scrooge did. And now, you're not going to be a grouch anymore!"

And I said, "Ho, ho, ho. No, no, no! That's not what happened. I was giving that silly book with the happy ending to the trash man just after you left, and he reminded me that Christmas is a holiday. Do you know what that means, Bird?"

Bird answered, "Sure. A holiday is a day when everyone is good and kind and celebrates...."

I had to interrupt. "No, no! It means that there's no trash pick-up that day, and I get to keep my wonderful trash one more day! What a gift! Merry Christmas, Bird!"

Gee, Oscar, that was a really grouchy story. Christmas isn't a grouchy time. It's a merry time! So let me tell a happy story, because that's what Christmas is all about! Here it is. It's called "A Wrap Session."

A WRAP SESSION

Early one Christmas Eve, not so long ago, everyone on Sesame Street gathered to wrap presents before the big Christmas party. But nobody had remembered to bring any wrapping paper or ribbons! Just then, Oscar the Grouch arrived with his gifts all wrapped up in newspaper and tied with bits of old string.

Betty Lou said, "Hey, Oscar, what a good idea! We don't need fancy paper and ribbons. We can wrap our presents with all kinds of things we find around the house!"

Just as we were finishing wrapping the gifts, Prairie Dawn looked out the window. She cried, "Oh, look! It's snowing! It's going to be a white Christmas after all! Let's go caroling!"

And that's just what we did. Here's what we sang.

GIFTS FOR THE TWELVE DAYS OF CHRISTMAS

FIRST DAY ....1 Delicious Cookie

SECOND DAY ....2 Baby Frogs

THIRD DAY ....3 Footballs

FOURTH DAY ....4 Woolly Bears

FIFTH DAY ....5 Argyle Socks

SIXTH DAY..............6 Rubber Duckies

SEVENTH DAY ....7 Rusty Trash Cans

EIGHTH DAY ....8 Counts a-Counting

NINTH DAY.............9 Pounds of Birdseed

TENTH DAY ....10 Wind-up Rabbits

ELEVENTH DAY......11 Broken Buildings

TWELFTH DAY ....?

MERRY CHRISTMAS,
EVERYBODY!

HAVE A GROUCHY
CHRISTMAS!

THE END!

Merry Christmas,
Everybody!

By **Constance Allen**
Illustrated by **David Prebenna**

FEATURING JIM HENSON'S SESAME STREET MUPPETS

On the day before Christmas, Grover was in a very big hurry.

"Merry Christmas, everybody!" he called as he rushed down Sesame Street. "I do not have time to stop right now because tomorrow is Christmas!"

"Merry Christmas, Grover!" called the Count. "Look at all the beautiful snowflakes! Do you want to count them with us?"

"I would love to," said Grover. "But I am a very busy monster today."

"Hello, Grover!" called Elmo. "Elmo and Rosita are making snow angels. Do you want to make one, too?"

"Not right now!" answered Grover. "I have
something very important to do."

"Oh, look!" said Grover. "Here is Nickles
Department Store. I have to stop in here for a moment.

"Pardon me. Excuse me. Clear the way, please."

"Merry Christmas, Mr. Santa Claus, sir," said
Grover. "I would like a red fire truck, please. I have
been a very well-behaved little monster. Thank you
very much, and now I really must be going.

"Oops! So *very* sorry, sir. Let me help you pick
up these packages. Merry Christmas, sir!"

"Yoo-hoo, Grover!" called Cookie Monster.
"Do you want a Christmas cookie?"
"No time for cookies now, thank you," said Grover.

"Merry Christmas, Grover!" called Snuffy.
"Do you want to ice-skate with Alice and me?"
"I cannot stop now!" answered Grover.

"Hey, Grover!" called Merry Monster. "Want to help us decorate the Christmas tree? Oscar helped make the ornaments."

"And I get to put the star on top when we're all finished!" said Big Bird.

"Thank you, everybody, but I am in a terrific rush!" said Grover, and he dashed away.

"Jingle bells, jingle bells,
Jingle all the way.
Oh, what fun it is to ride
In a one-horse open sleigh!"

"Merry Christmas, Grover!" called Bert. "Want to come Christmas caroling with us?"

"Thank you, but I must be dashing through the snow," answered Grover as he ran.

"Merry Christmas, Grover!" said Telly. "Look at the wrapping paper we made in play group. Isn't it neat? Want to come wrap presents with me?"

"Thank you, Telly, but there is no time to lose!" called Grover. "Clear the way, please!"

"Oh, joy! Here I am at last!" said Grover when he got to the post office. "I hope my cousin Fred will receive this present in time for Christmas."

Grover hurried up to the counter and said to the clerk, "Do you want to know what I am sending to my cousin who lives in Florida? If I tell you, will you promise not to tell him?

"I am sending him . . .

"SNOWBALLS!"

A Grouch's
Christmas

By **Michaela Muntean**
Illustrated by **Tom Leigh**

FEATURING JIM HENSON'S SESAME STREET MUPPETS

It was the day before Christmas and Elmo was helping his mother make Christmas cookies. Elmo watched his mother roll the dough out on the countertop. Then he cut out shapes in the dough with cookie cutters and sprinkled them with colored sugar.

Elmo stood in front of the oven door and watched as the cookies turned golden brown.

When the cookies came out of the oven, Elmo's mother said, "You may try one, Elmo. But we have to save the rest for our Christmas guests. This year you are big enough to pass the plate of cookies yourself."

"Okay, Mommy! And Elmo will tell everyone that Elmo helped make them!"

Elmo picked out a reindeer-shaped cookie. "Mmmm…these are good! Cookie Monster will love them."

As Elmo's mother was putting away the flour and sugar, she glanced out the kitchen window and said, "Look, Elmo! It's snowing!"

"Oh, boy! Mommy, may Elmo please go outside to play?"

"Yes, dear. Let's put on your coat and boots. Here is a big scarf to tie around your neck. Keep dry and don't stay out too long."

"Okay, Mommy!"

And Elmo ran out the door and down Sesame Street
to build a snowmonster. He saw the footprints that his
boots made in the new snow.

The snow was as white and fine as the flour Elmo's
mother sprinkled on the counter for the cookie dough.
Snowflakes drifted down and clung to Elmo's hat and
scarf. He opened his mouth to catch some more.

All along Sesame Street, Elmo saw his friends getting
ready for Christmas. Ernie and Bert were carrying a
Christmas tree. Luis was stringing colored lights in the
window of the Fix-It Shop. Big Bird was decorating a
little Christmas tree. Herry Monster had dressed up
like Santa Claus, and he was ringing a bell and
collecting toys and food for needy families. The Count
was counting snowflakes as they fell.

"One beautiful snowflake! Two beautiful snowflakes!
Three, four, five, six, seven, eight...so many beautiful
snowflakes! Wonderful!"

"Merry Christmas, everybody!" Elmo shouted.

"Merry Christmas, Elmo!" his friends called back.

Elmo passed by Oscar's trash can. "Merry Christmas, Oscar!"

"Humph! I hate Christmas!" said Oscar.

Elmo stopped suddenly. He lifted up the earflaps of his cap and said, "Would you please say that again, Oscar? Elmo doesn't think he heard right."

"Of course I will. I'll say it again and again and again. I hate Christmas. I hate Christmas. I hate Christmas!"

"But how could you hate Christmas, Oscar? There's nothing about Christmas to hate!"

"Oh, yes there is. There's all that ho-ho-ho-ing and fa-la-la-ing. There's everyone going around smiling and being cheerful and giving each other nice presents. This is the worst time of the year for grouches."

"Oh, Oscar! There are things about Christmas even a grouch would like."

"Name one," said Oscar.

Elmo thought for a moment. "Cookies! Elmo just helped his mommy make Christmas cookies."

"Were they sardine cookies with chocolate icing?" Oscar asked.

"No. They were sugar cookies shaped like stars and Christmas trees and reindeer. Elmo cut them out all by himself!"

Oscar scowled. "Yucch! They sound awful!"

"Just wait, Oscar! Elmo will be right back! Elmo is going to find a *zillion* reasons for Oscar to like Christmas!"

"Don't worry. I'm not going anywhere until the holidays are over!" grumbled Oscar. And he disappeared inside his trash can and slammed the lid down with a crash.

Elmo forgot all about building snowmonsters. He went looking for reasons for Oscar to like Christmas. If he couldn't find a zillion, he was sure he could find a few.

First Elmo stopped at Big Bird's nest. Elmo told him what he wanted to do. Big Bird said, "I've got an idea! I'll meet you at Oscar's trash can in one hour."

Next Elmo stopped to visit Ernie and Bert. They said they'd help, too. Elmo stopped to see Herry and then The Count. They all agreed to meet at Oscar's.

Elmo raced back home and told his mother what he wanted to do.

"That sounds disgusting," she said. But she helped anyway.

When everything was ready, Elmo hurried to Oscar's can.
His friends were there, just as they had promised.

"Merry Christmas, Oscar!" Elmo called as he knocked on
the trash can lid.

Oscar popped out of his can. "I told you, I hate Christmas!"

Elmo laughed. "And Elmo told *you* he was going to find a
zillion reasons why you would like it."

"So, did you?" Oscar asked.

"No, Oscar. But Elmo found a few really good ones!"

Ernie and Bert handed Oscar a little Christmas tree. It was decorated with old tin cans, orange peels, and bits of raggedy string.

"That's not a bad-looking Christmas tree. You guys decorated it just for me, huh?"

"See, Oscar," said Elmo. "That's one thing to like about Christmas!"

"Well, thanks, you guys."

"I like Christmas because it's a time for families to get together." said Big Bird. "Tomorrow my Granny Bird is coming to visit."

"So?"

"So, maybe Grundgetta would come and visit you if you invited her, Oscar," suggested Big Bird.

"Hmmm…." said Oscar. "That's not the worst idea I've ever heard. Grundgetta and I could sit around complaining and grumbling."

"You see? That's *another* nice thing about Christmas — it's a time for families to enjoy themselves," said Big Bird.

Herry said, "I like Christmas because it's about sharing and helping others. Today I collected toys and food for families who need them. Tonight Grover and I are going to deliver them. You don't happen to have anything to share, do you, Oscar?"

"Just a minute." Oscar disappeared into his trash can.

He came back a few seconds later. "Here. Maybe someone could use this," said Oscar, as he handed Herry a brand-new, red-and-white-striped scarf.

"Why, thank you, Oscar!" said Herry. "I'm sure someone could use it. Doesn't it feel good to help someone else?"

"I suppose so. It sure feels good to get rid of that scarf. It's too clean and it doesn't have one moth hole in it. I wouldn't want Grundgetta to see it if she comes tomorrow."

"Oscar, Elmo made twelve reasons for you to like Christmas!" said Elmo, "Here are a dozen sardine Christmas cookies with chocolate icing. Merry Christmas, Oscar!"

"There is something else to like about Christmas," said The Count.

"What's that?" asked Oscar.

"Your friends! When you count your blessings, count your friends. Let me count them for you… one friend… two friends…"

"Never mind, Count! I can do it," said Oscar.

Oscar was quiet for a minute. Finally he turned to
Elmo and said, "Okay, I give up! You were right, Elmo.
Christmas isn't so bad after all."

Then Oscar took a bite of a sardine cookie. "And
these cookies are delicious. Thanks, Elmo. And,
Merry Christmas."

Then everybody began to sing, and Oscar sang the
fa-la-la-ing part the loudest.